THE INCREDIBLES

Ladybird

DURING the golden age of the Supers, Mr Incredible was the world's greatest hero. With the power of Super strength, he caught criminals and stopped disasters. He protected the public from harm.

Mr Incredible's greatest fan was a boy called Buddy.
He desperately wanted to be a Super like his hero.
Buddy decided to change his name to Incrediboy
and he even invented some rocket boots that
allowed him to fly. He asked Mr Incredible if he

could be his side kick but Mr Incredible told Buddy
that fancy boots didn't make someone into a
Super. Supers were born, not made.

Mr Incredible
married another
Super, Elastigirl. The
two Supers loved each
other and the future
seemed bright… until
disaster struck.

People started to sue the Supers – some of them claimed they hadn't wanted to be saved at all! The government told the Supers to stop being heroes. They had to go into hiding and live like normal people.

So Mr Incredible became boring, average Bob Parr, and Elastigirl became Helen. They had a shy daughter, Violet, who could turn invisible and create force fields, a Super-fast son named Dash, and a baby called Jack-Jack who seemed to have no Super powers at all. With all these Super powers, family meals could get chaotic. Controlling Super kids was tough.

Helen adjusted very well to normal life and focused all her efforts on the kids. Bob worked in a boring job at an insurance company. He desperately missed being a Super. Bob just couldn't help dreaming of the past. Occasionally, he would blow his cover by using his powers in public. Then the whole family would have to be relocated and start all over again.

One night, Bob went out with his friend Lucius. In the Super era Lucius was known as Frozone, literally the coolest Super of all! They were tuned into the police radio – Bob was listening to reports of crimes in progress. He was hoping to save someone – just like the good old days. When he heard about a fire at a nearby apartment building, Bob convinced Lucius they should go and help.

"We're gonna get caught," said Lucius.

The two Supers saved several people – but in order to escape the fire, they had to break into the jeweller's next door.

A policeman thought they were thieves, so Lucius used his Super powers to freeze him, and the two Supers escaped.

Nearby, a mysterious woman watched them from her car.

Next day at work, Bob wanted to help someone who was being mugged but his boss wouldn't let him go. Bob was so frustrated at not being allowed to help that he gave his boss a tiny push, but it carried all of Bob's Super strength. His boss crashed through five walls, and Bob lost his job.

Bob was worried. He didn't want to tell Helen he was fired, but what could he do without a job?

At home in his den, Bob was clearing out his briefcase. Suddenly, a computer fell out! On the screen was the woman who had been secretly watching him the night before.

"My name is Mirage," she said. "I represent a top secret division of the government. A highly experimental robot has escaped our control… "

She had a very special top secret mission for Mr Incredible!

Mirage told Bob that if he could stop the malfunctioning Omnidroid battle robot before it caused any damage, he'd be paid three times his yearly salary! Bob accepted. He needed the money – but more importantly he needed the adventure. Bob knew Helen wouldn't approve, so he told her he was going on a business trip.

Bob was taken to the island of Nomanisan, where he and Mirage discussed his mission.

"Shut it down. Do it quickly," he confirmed.

"And don't die," added Mirage.

Mr Incredible soon encountered the robot, and the fight began. The Omnidroid was a fast learner when it came to defending itself, but in the end Mr Incredible tricked it into self-destruction.

Mirage and her boss watched the Omnidroid's defeat.

"Surprising," said her boss.

After a celebration dinner with Mirage, Bob flew home. He was excited about getting back into Super work. He began to lose weight, bought a new car and even played with the kids! Things were looking up. But he'd ripped his suit, so he decided to visit Edna Mode – the former fashion designer for the Supers. She agreed to mend the old suit for sentimental reasons, but insisted on making him a new bold, dramatic outfit!

The new suit arrived just in time. Mirage had a new assignment for Bob. "Another conference," he told Helen. "Short notice but duty calls!"

As Bob flew back to the island, Helen had discovered a blonde hair on his jacket. She wondered where he was **really** going…

Mr Incredible got quite a shock when he arrived for his briefing. He was attacked by a new and improved Omnidroid!

This time the robot was unbeatable. As it defeated the hero, a stranger in a black costume appeared.

"It's too much for Mr Incredible," he gloated. "I went through quite a few Supers to make it worthy to fight you. But you're worth it. After all, I'm your biggest fan."

"Buddy?" Mr Incredible said. He barely recognised his former number-one fan.

"My name's not Buddy, I'm Syndrome! And now I have a weapon that only I can defeat…"

As Mr Incredible tried to escape, Syndrome froze him in his immobi-ray.

"Who's Super now?" he yelled. But then he lost control and accidentally flung Mr Incredible off a waterfall! Syndrome threw a bomb after him but Mr Incredible found safety in an underwater cave. Syndrome sent a probe to find him. But the hero hid behind the remains of Gazerbeam – a Super

who had died battling the Omnidroid. Just before he died, Gazerbeam had used his laser vision to etch the word KRONOS on the cave wall. What could it mean? Bob wondered.

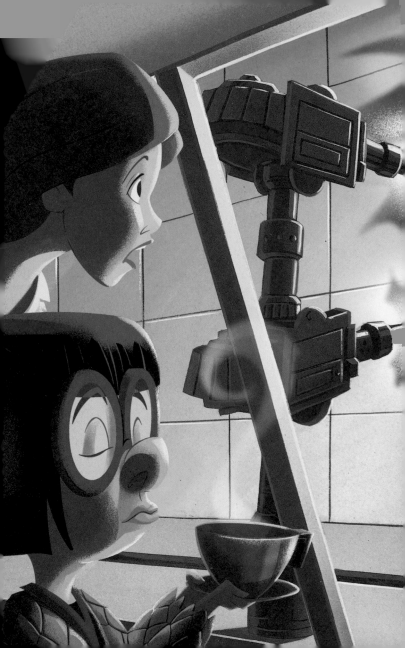

Meanwhile, Helen had found Bob's newly mended suit. She knew that Edna must have fixed it, so she went straight to her to find out what Bob was up to.

Edna was thrilled to see Helen. She'd so enjoyed making and testing Bob's new suit that she'd made one for Helen too – and one each for Violet, Dash and Jack-Jack! Each new suit came with a homing device for handy tracking.

But Helen was very upset.

"You helped my husband resume secret hero work behind my back?"

"I assumed you knew, darling," Edna protested.

Helen phoned Bob's work – and learned he'd been fired almost two months ago. Where was he? Edna passed Helen the homing device that would locate him.

Meanwhile, back on the island, Bob sneaked into Syndrome's base. Using the password KRONOS he hacked into the computer – and discovered Syndrome's plan.

Syndrome had killed many Supers perfecting his Omnidroid. Now, he planned to set the robot loose in the city. No one would be able to stop it.

Suddenly, Mr Incredible's homing device went off! Now Helen knew where he was – but so did the island's security. They shot out great sticky globules to catch him. Mr Incredible was trapped!

Back on the mainland Helen knew she must find her husband. She realised she would only be able to do it if she became Elastigirl!

Elastigirl followed the homing signal in a borrowed jet. She soon found that Violet and Dash had left Jack-Jack at home with a babysitter and stowed away on the jet! They had also found their Super suits! As they approached the island, the jet was attacked by missiles. Elastigirl told Violet to create a force field around the plane. But Violet was hesitant – she didn't think she could make one that big.

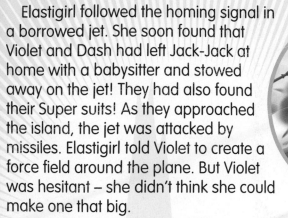

In his prison cell, Mr Incredible listened to the attack on his family with horror.

"Target destroyed," came a voice from a speaker.

"You'll get over it," Syndrome sneered.

A desperate Mr Incredible grabbed Mirage.

"Release me now, or I'll crush her!" he said.

"Go ahead," said Syndrome.

He knew that Mr Incredible could never do such a thing, no matter how upset he was.

Defeated, the hero let Mirage go.

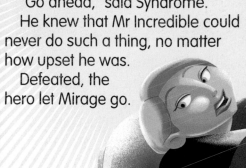

But Mr Incredible's family was still alive. Elastigirl had stretched herself around Violet and Dash to protect them, just as the missile blew the jet out of the sky. Then she had made herself into a parachute and floated, with her kids, down to the water below.

Elastigirl stretched into the shape of a boat, while Dash pushed her and Violet to shore by kicking his speedy legs. They soon found safety in a cave.

"I'm going to look for your father," Elastigirl told her children. "If anything goes wrong, use your powers… When the time comes, you'll know what to do."

After Helen left, the cave suddenly filled with a huge ball of fire. Dash and Violet fled; they only just escaped! The fire was the rocket exhaust from Syndrome's base. He had launched the Omnidroid towards the city!

At headquarters, Mirage had decided to set Mr Incredible free. She was angry that Syndrome had challenged the hero to hurt her and she wanted him to know that his family was still alive.

Mr Incredible was so happy to hear this news that he hugged Mirage. But just then Elastigirl burst in! She punched Mirage from across the room. Mr Incredible tried to explain that Mirage was trying to help him. But Elastigirl was too angry to believe him.

"Where are the kids?" asked Mr Incredible.

"They might've triggered the alert," said Mirage, rubbing her jaw. "Security's been sent into the jungle!"

Syndrome's guards had indeed found Violet and Dash. They chased the two young Supers on velocipods. Vi protected herself and Dash with a force field. Then Dash began to run. They raced through the jungle in the protective ball, rolling at top speed.

Mr Incredible and Elastigirl found their kids when they were bowled over by them.

Together, the family fought off Syndrome's guards. They made a top team. But suddenly Syndrome arrived and locked the Incredibles in his immobi-ray.

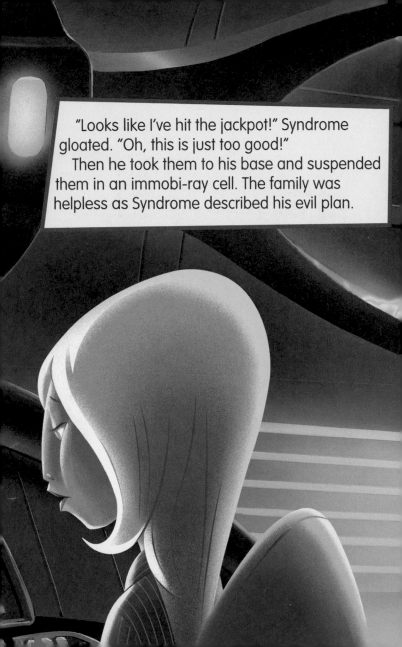

"Looks like I've hit the jackpot!" Syndrome gloated. "Oh, this is just too good!"

Then he took them to his base and suspended them in an immobi-ray cell. The family was helpless as Syndrome described his evil plan.

"The robot will emerge dramatically, do some damage, and just when all hope is lost..." the villain explained. "Syndrome will save the day!" He sneered at Mr Incredible. "I'll be a bigger hero than you ever were!"

"You killed off real heroes so that you could pretend to be one!" said Mr Incredible.

"I've got a city to save!" Syndrome cackled as he took off for the mainland.

"I'm sorry," Mr Incredible told his family. "I've been a lousy father. So obsessed with being undervalued that I undervalued all of you." He sighed. "**You** are my greatest adventure."

But even as he spoke, Vi was creating a force field, allowing her to escape the energy beams and set her family free. Soon the Incredibles were back in action!

Mirage helped the family escape from the island in a rocket. They flew towards the city where the Omnidroid was already destroying everything it could find.

The people of the city were terrified.

"Someone needs to teach this hunk of metal a few manners!" Syndrome told the crowd. Sneakily he worked the robot's remote control and removed the Omnidroid's arm. The crowd cheered, and Syndrome loved it.

But the Omnidroid was a learning robot, and it realised Syndrome was controlling it. It zapped the remote and knocked Syndrome out.

Luckily, the Incredibles had just crash-landed in a van that Elastigirl had held to the rocket. Then Mr Incredible announced he would fight the robot alone. When Elastigirl objected, Mr Incredible begged her, "I can't lose you again," he said. "I'm not strong enough."

Elastigirl smiled gently. "If we work together, you won't have to be."

The Supers fought as a team. Mr Incredible's old pal Frozone helped them too.

Still the Omnidroid proved to be quite a foe – that is, until Mr Incredible remembered that the only thing that could defeat the Omnidroid was itself. He grabbed a rocket-loaded claw that had fallen from the robot. Elastigirl, Frozone and the kids pushed buttons on the remote control while Mr Incredible aimed the claw so it pointed at the Omnidroid. Just then Elastigirl found the right button. The rocket ripped the robot apart. The city was saved!

Syndrome recovered to find everyone cheering the Supers! No one cared about him! Furious, he crept away.

When the Incredibles returned home they found that a replacement babysitter had come for Jack-Jack – Syndrome!

"You stole my future," said Syndrome. "I'm returning the favour! Don't worry, I'll be a good mentor… and in time, who knows? He might make a good sidekick!"

Syndrome blasted a hole in the roof and flew off with Jack-Jack towards his waiting jet. But Jack-Jack was upset. He began to cry and wail. **Then** he began to transform using Super powers!

Suddenly Syndrome was no longer holding a sweet baby, but a flaming monster! Jack-Jack tore through Syndrome's rocket boots. Syndrome quickly dropped him and raced for his nearby jet.

Mr Incredible used his Super strength to throw
Elastigirl into the air. She caught Jack-Jack and
then stretched out into a parachute to bring him
safely back to the ground.

"This isn't the end of it!" Syndrome raged.

But he was wrong. Mr Incredible picked up a car
and threw it at the jet. Syndrome was jolted by the
blast. His cape got caught in one of the engines.
And with one last yell, Syndrome was gone.

As the jet exploded, Vi protected her family with
a force field. Their house was destroyed by falling
wreckage – but the Incredibles were safe.

"That's my girl," said Elastigirl to her daughter.

With the danger to the city over, the Incredibles returned to their undercover life. But fitting in was just a little easier now. Vi was more confident in herself and Dash was even allowed to use a **little** of his Super speed by running on the school team. He was careful to always come in a close second.

But as the Super family left school sports day, the ground began to rumble. A monstrous machine broke out of the earth, with a menacing figure riding on top of it.

"Behold the Underminer!" the figure cried. "All will tremble before me!"

It was time for the family to put on their masks and change into their Super suits. This was a job for the Incredibles!